THE
MOON MONSTERS

Douglas Hill

Illustrated by
JEREMY FORD

HEINEMANN·LONDON

First published in 1984 by Heinemann Young Books
an imprint of Egmont Children's Books Limited
Michelin House, 81 Fulham Rd, London SW3 6RB

ISBN 0 434 93024 5

Reprinted 1985, 1989, 1991, 1995 and 1998
Text © Douglas Hill 1984
Illustrations © Jeremy Ford 1984

Printed in Italy by Olivotto

A school pack of BANANAS 1-6
is available from
Heinemann Educational Books
ISBN 0 435 00100 0

1. Space holiday

Paul Carder glanced over at his father, and sighed. Then he turned back to the viewport, to stare out at the endless blackness of space, speckled with countless stars.

He sighed again. It was a marvellous sight, and he had always wanted to see it – which was why he had been so excited when his father had invited him along on this two-week trip into deep space, during a school holiday.

But now, halfway through the trip, Paul was bored.

There just wasn't much for a

nine-year-old boy to *do* on a small Surveyor spaceship. He couldn't move around easily in the cramped living area. He had watched all the vid-tapes that he had brought, some of them twice. And most of the time his father was too busy to talk, to tell the stories about alien worlds that Paul loved to hear.

He glanced again at his father, who was working at his maps and computer diagrams as usual. Paul felt a little guilty for being bored. His father was an expert on astro-geography. Paul was very proud of him and it was a special treat for Paul to go along on one of his father's trips into space to study the stars.

All the same . . . What he'd really like, Paul thought, was to *see* one of those alien worlds of his father's stories. Maybe even land on it . . .

He turned back to the viewport – and then sat up. The stars seemed suddenly to be wheeling crazily, as if the whole galaxy was turning.

But he knew better. It was their ship that was moving, picking up speed, swinging away in a different direction.

He looked quickly around, and saw that his father was smiling at him.

'I thought that would brighten you up,' he said.

'Where are we going?' Paul asked.

'To a star nearby,' his father replied, 'that has a couple of planets around it. One of the planets is huge – ten times the size of Earth. I thought you'd like to see it.'

'Can we land?' Paul asked excitedly. But the excitement faded at his father's shake of the head.

'Not a chance, I'm afraid,' Mr Carder said. 'It's mostly gas and liquid, probably deadly. But we'll get fairly close. It'll be worth seeing.'

2. Forced landing

THE PLANET WAS very much worth seeing. Even from a long way away, it looked gigantic, glowing with livid reds and yellows. And the surface seemed to be boiling, as enormous storms swept through the swirling clouds of gases above it.

Paul saw that there was a second planet in the distance, which seemed dull in comparison with the giant glowing one. Then his father pointed in another direction, and Paul saw a third sphere, smaller than the other two, but bright and solid-looking.

'Seems this huge planet has a moon,' Mr Carder said. 'A good-sized one, too.'

He was looking at the screen of one of his scanners, which told him a great deal about distant objects in space.

'It's interesting,' he said. 'There seems to be life on this moon. Animals, plants, lots of different kinds.'

'Can we go closer?' Paul asked.

'I think we will,' his father said.

He touched the controls and they hurtled away towards the moon. Paul gazed out with delight. The moon was

nearly as big as Earth. And, like Earth, it had oceans and mountains, broad plains and deep forests, all brightly lit by the glow of the giant planet, like a second sun in the sky.

'Couldn't we land, Dad?' Paul begged. 'Just for a minute?'

'We'd better not, Paul,' his father said. 'We don't know what's down there. We'll just fly over, as low as we can.'

They were now above a large stretch of forest, so crowded with strange trees and brush that it was more like a jungle. Mr Carder sent the ship lower, until it was flying just above the tangle of green-brown leaves. And Paul stared

down, wishing that the tangle wasn't so thick, so that he could see the ground, and maybe an alien creature.

Then his wish came true – in a way that filled him with terror.

A huge flock of flying creatures came plunging up towards them. Each creature was twice as big as the biggest bird on Earth. They had vast bat-like

wings, and wrinkled, purplish hide.
Their long fangs and claws glittered like
shiny metal.

Paul's father tried to swerve the ship,
to avoid them. There were so many that
the sky seemed to have turned dark
purple. The ship jolted as some of the
winged monsters bounced off it. Then

there was a loud scraping noise as the
ship grazed the top of a very tall tree.

'We'll have to go down!' his father
shouted. 'Before these things damage
the ship!'

As he spoke, the trees below them
seemed to open. The spaceship had come
to a wide, grassy clearing in the jungle.

Mr Carder dropped the ship down towards it, and with relief Paul saw that the flying things were not pursuing them, but were flapping away higher into the sky.

As the ship settled on to the clearing, Paul's father managed a grin.

'You got your wish, Paul,' he said. 'We've landed. Get your spacesuit on, and we'll go and see if the ship's come to any harm.'

3. Into the jungle

PAUL GOT INTO his spacesuit in record time, and followed his father out, wide-eyed with excitement. He was standing on an alien world—with an alien sky, strange alien grass, and over there a shadowy alien jungle.

More than anything, Paul wanted to go over and peer into those jungle shadows. Maybe even walk into them. Just a step or two . . .

His father's voice came through the small radio in Paul's space-helmet. 'The ship seems fine,' he said. 'Let's check up top.'

Each of their spacesuits was equipped

with a jet-pack – like a personal rocket, using special fuel. When Paul's father touched a switch on his belt, a burst of gases jetted from the pack, lifting him into the air, to soar smoothly up on to the top of the ship. Paul flicked his own belt-switch and followed.

The upper surface of the ship also seemed unharmed. So their jet-packs brought them gently back down to the ground.

'Now we can get out of here,' Mr Carder said with relief.

'Dad, couldn't we go into the jungle?' Paul asked. 'Just for a minute?'

His father looked doubtful. 'It could be dangerous, Paul. We've got nothing to protect ourselves with.'

Paul knew that very well. His father hated guns, and hated the way that some spacemen from Earth would shoot alien creatures without a thought. He believed that you should stay away from places that might be dangerous, rather than shooting your way out of trouble because you had been careless or stupid.

But Paul was not to be put off so easily. 'We've got the jet-packs, Dad,' he said. 'We could just have a quick look, and maybe take some pictures.'

He held his breath. His father was a keen photographer, who took wonderful pictures of alien places with his 3-D camera. Paul was sure that the mention of pictures would bring him round.

He was right. 'You win,' Mr Carder said with a smile. 'Just a quick look. Go and get the camera.'

Paul scrambled happily into the ship, and returned in seconds with the long-lensed 3-D camera. Then they moved towards the tangle of colourful plants at the edge of the jungle.

4. Nightmare flight

'STAY CLOSE, PAUL,' his father warned him. 'And keep your eyes open, every moment.'

Paul gulped and nodded. He was still feeling excited, but also a little frightened. Even a few steps beyond the clearing, the jungle seemed to have swallowed them up in its dim, spooky

depths. The vines and branches reached out like grasping fingers, and there were strange rustlings in the thick brush.

Yet the only creature they saw near the clearing was a small green-furred thing with six legs, that glared at them from the branches with tiny red eyes. Paul's father raised the camera, but the creature fled. They followed it for half a kilometre, deep into the jungle, before it would sit still long enough to have its picture taken.

But then Mr Carder felt that they had gone far enough, and they set off back to the clearing.

Until they saw that their way was
barred.

The barrier stretched across the path
that they had taken only moments
before. It was made of glistening strands,
like a spider's web. Except this barrier
was shaped more like a square of wire
netting. And it was big enough to trap
very large creatures. Even human
beings.

Then Mr Carder glanced to one side, and went white. 'Jump, Paul!' he yelled.

Paul had only a glimpse of the thing rushing out of the brush. It was as shiny as a beetle, long and many-legged like a caterpillar—but twice as large as Paul. Each stubby leg ended in a sharp claw, and its jaws were like two curved blades, clashing together.

Paul's hand hit his belt-switch, and both jet-packs flared. The leap took them crashing away through dense brush, and they were both breathing hard when they landed.

'We can circle around, to get back to the ship,' said Paul's father. 'We should be all right now.'

But their return to the clearing became a nightmare journey.

They had taken only a few steps when they had to leap away again on their

jet-packs. Out of the brush slithered a
creature with a flat lumpy body, a long
scaly neck, and a hissing beak-mouth
that opened wide as it charged them.

When that jump ended, they landed
almost on top of a large, snarling, grey
thing with huge hind legs and small
clawed forelegs. It had tentacles around
its head, like a squid, and the head was

nearly all mouth, and the mouth fangs.

They jumped again, in panic. And again they jumped, as a cat-like creature larger than a lion, covered in long sharp spines like thorns, prowled towards them hungrily. Again and again they jumped, as more monsters appeared. They seemed to Paul to be behind every tree and bush. Hairy monsters with many legs, slimy monsters with no legs, hard-shelled monsters, scaly monsters, slithering or hopping or crawling or bounding monsters, all of them with fangs and claws. . .

But at last they came to rest, after another leap on their jet-packs, at a spot that seemed free of alien horrors. Paul was trembling and near to tears as he watched his father grimly study the jungle around them.

'We should be near the clearing now,' his father said. 'And there weren't any creatures near the edge of it.' He swung an arm around Paul's shoulders. 'Ready to go on?'

Paul nodded faintly, wanting nothing else at that moment except to be inside the safe haven of the spaceship. And if we get there, he promised himself, I'll never ever feel bored again.

They moved forward – walking, because they had nearly used up the fuel in their jet-packs. That frightened Paul, too. So he felt a huge relief when he saw a bright patch of sky that showed they were coming to the clearing.

Mr Carder halted, suddenly tense. And as Paul peered nervously through the leafy bushes at the clearing's edge, he felt as if his body had turned to ice.

Their ship was surrounded. Not by
monstrous beasts, but by quite different
creatures. Alien beings.

5. The trap

THEY WERE SHAPED more or less like
humans, but were very tall, with
strangely flattened faces, and bright blue

skin. There were eight of them, wearing what seemed to be uniforms. And the objects in their hands looked like weapons – weird alien rifles.

'Dad . . .' Paul said, in a small, terrified voice.

'Stay still,' his father said. 'They haven't seen us.'

Paul didn't need to be told to stay still. He was too frightened to move. And he was grateful for the curtain of leaves that hid them from the menacing alien group.

'What'll we do?' he almost wailed.

'Depends on what they do,' his father replied. 'Maybe they'll go away, in a while.'

So they waited, crouched at the clearing's edge, and watched the armed aliens. But the blue-skinned beings looked as if they were there to stay. They stood quietly around the ship, weapons ready, watching the jungle and clearly waiting for the owners of the spaceship to return.

An hour went by, and then another. Paul grew more and more frightened – not only of the aliens in the clearing ahead of them, but of all the horrifying monsters that might be creeping up behind them. Worse still, it was starting to get dark.

As the shadows around them grew blacker, Paul's father drew him back away from the clearing. 'We have to find a safer place to spend the night,' he said.

'Maybe the aliens will be gone by morning.'

Paul nodded numbly, and they crept away back into the jungle.

Soon they found a hiding place that looked fairly safe, even in that jungle night; a giant tree, with a dense network of branches far from the ground. Their jet-packs lifted them into the tree, where criss-crossing branches made a natural platform.

Paul stared around. 'I hope there aren't any monsters that climb trees.'

His father managed a faint smile, and lifted the almost-forgotten 3-D camera. 'If there are,' he said, 'I'll beat them off with this.' He squeezed Paul's shoulder gently. 'Try to sleep. I'll keep watch.'

Paul settled back. He was worn out after all the terrors of the day, but the knot of fear inside him made him sure that he would never close his eyes. He was just as sure of this when, five minutes later, he drifted off to sleep.

It seemed only another five minutes afterwards that he felt a hand shaking him. He awoke with a jerk, staring wildly around.

'What . . . ?' he almost yelled.

'No monsters,' his father's voice said calmly. 'It's dawn, that's all. Let's go and look at our ship.'

They jetted back down to the ground, moving stiffly at first as they crept

forward through the brush, eerie and
ghostly in the grey light of dawn. The
knot of fear grew tighter inside Paul, as
they came to the clearing.

But then it seemed to disappear, and
Paul shouted aloud with joy.

The aliens were gone. Their ship stood
alone in the empty clearing.

They burst out of the jungle, and
began to hurry across the clearing. But
they were only halfway to the ship when
they heard a thunderous bellow behind
them.

They turned, and froze in horror. It was a massive beast, tall as an elephant and twice as wide. It moved on eight legs, as thick as trees, half-hidden by a shaggy coat of dark red hair. And the vast head was armed with what looked like a forest of wickedly sharp horns.

The monster bellowed again, and the ground trembled as it began to lumber towards them.

'Jump!' Mr Carder shouted.

Paul hit his belt-switch, soaring away in a long curving flight towards the ship. As he touched down, he looked back. And his heart seemed to stop.

His father had not moved. He was fumbling with his belt-switch, out there in the open. The monster, horned head lowered, was charging at full gallop.

Desperately, Mr Carder began to run as the huge creature thundered towards him. And Paul, horrified, realised what had happened. His father's jet-pack had run out of fuel.

Paul knew that he could not outrun the monster. Those terrible horns would be upon him in seconds.

Mr Carder, too, saw that he could not escape. He turned to face the monster, gripping the 3-D camera like a club. But Paul knew that it would be no more use than a twig against the enormous beast. And the monster was only a few metres away. . .

Then the creature planted its eight feet, and slid to a sudden and complete halt.

Paul gaped, unable to believe his eyes. His father too seemed frozen with disbelief. The monster scarcely looked at him. It shook its great head, snorted, then turned and ambled slowly away.

'*Dad*!' Paul shrieked.

Mr Carder turned and waved, looking dazed, and hurried towards the ship. 'I don't know what . . .' he began to say – but then he broke off.

Paul heard a familiar whine of machinery, and whirled around, new panic flashing through him. The sound was that of the ship's airlock, opening. And out from the airlock were stepping eight tall, blue-skinned figures, weapons in their hands.

The aliens had got into the ship, to set a trap.

6. The Wardens

PAUL SHRANK BACK, and felt his father's arm go around his shoulders.

'Keep still,' warned the alien in the lead. 'Lower your weapon.'

Even through his terror, Paul felt amazed. The aliens were speaking the language of Earth.

'We have no weapon,' Mr Carder said calmly.

The alien leader stepped forward, jerking the camera from his grasp. 'How many creatures have you destroyed with this?' he snapped.

'It's a camera,' Mr Carder said. 'It takes pictures, but does no harm.'

The aliens seemed to ignore his words, and crowded forward menacingly. Paul shrank away even farther, certain that he and his father would be killed.

But the alien leader had been inspecting the camera. Two deft movements of his hands had opened it up.

'The off-worlder speaks the truth,' he said. 'This cannot be a weapon.'

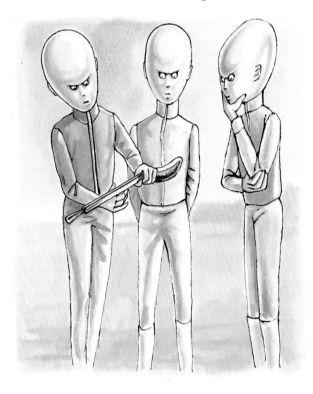

As if by magic, the threatening tension seemed to vanish. The aliens moved back, peering curiously at the camera. Then the alien leader turned to Mr Carder and Paul.

'We apologize,' he said. 'We believed you to be illegal hunters trespassing on our moon.'

Mr Carder and Paul stared. 'Perhaps you would explain what you're talking about,' Paul's father said.

And so the alien, who said his name was Alend, explained.

He and the others came from the second planet, the smaller world that Paul had seen near the huge gas and liquid planet. The people of that world were highly civilized, gentle and peace-loving. But long ago, when they had not been so peaceful, their favourite sport had been hunting. Now, they saw

no sport in using advanced weapons to
slaughter other creatures, but they still
enjoyed the excitement of stalking wild
beasts, especially large and dangerous
ones.

So they had made this moon, which
was called Ishm, into a place where they
could hunt.

'I don't get it,' Mr Carder said. 'Your
people don't like killing animals, yet
they have made this place into a . . . a
game reserve, for hunting?'

The alien called Alend nodded.
'Exactly. But very *special* hunting.'

The monsters of Ishm were not truly alive, he said. They were robot creatures, with computers as their brains. And they were programmed to behave like wild beasts, even to be fierce and threatening.

'But as you saw,' Alend said, 'a beast will never really attack. It stops, and goes away harmlessly.'

Mr Carder looked dazed. 'But do you *shoot* them?'

'In a way,' Alend said. 'Observe.'

He raised his strange rifle and aimed it

at the huge, horned creature, which was still wandering around the clearing. Paul jumped as a beam of bright blue light flashed from the rifle, striking the beast's vast, hairy side.

The beast seemed to freeze, rigid and unmoving, as if it had been turned into a statue.

'The beam shuts off the computer inside the creature,' Alend said. 'It will be still for a few moments. Then the computer will start up again, and it will return to normal.'

Mr Carder slowly shook his head. 'All this, just so people can go hunting.'

'Only in this way,' Alend replied, 'can our hunting be sport, rather than slaughter.'

'Quite right,' Mr Carder said firmly. 'I dislike killing as much as you do.'

'Then you are welcome here,' Alend said. 'We are the Wardens of Ishm. We look after the creatures, and the hunters – including many invited visitors from other worlds. And we guard Ishm against off-worlders who come without permission, to destroy the beasts.'

'Which is what you thought we were,' Mr Carder said.

As the alien nodded, Paul found his voice. 'How did you learn our language?' he asked.

'You are not the first Earth people to visit Ishm,' Alend told him. 'But they have kept it a secret, as we ask you to do.

We do not want visits from the more violent and destructive of your kind.'

Paul and his father promised to tell no one. Then the group chatted for a few more moments, and the aliens posed for

a few pictures. But finally Mr Carder said that it was time to leave.

'If you like,' Alend said, 'you could stay a while, and explore Ishm.'

'Could we, Dad?' Paul said quickly. 'Please?'

His father shook his head. 'I've still got a lot to do in space on this trip, Paul.' But as Paul's face fell, he smiled. 'Still, there'll be another school holiday soon. And by then, I'll need a holiday too. Maybe a nice . . . hunting trip?'

'Whenever you wish,' Alend said.

'Great!' Paul said, beaming. But his face fell again. 'Only . . . if we have to keep all this a secret, I'll never be able to tell them at school about my fantastic holiday!'

'No, you won't,' his father said sternly. Then he grinned. 'You'll just have to say that you went flying around in space with your father, and were bored out of your mind.'